Finger Rhymes

collected and illustrated by

MARC BROWN

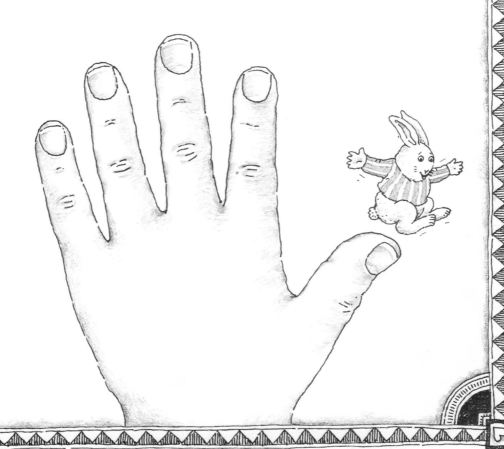

A UNICORN BOOK   E. P. DUTTON   NEW YORK

for Emilie,
my editor, teacher and friend

Copyright © 1980 by Marc Brown

All rights reserved.

Library of Congress Cataloging in Publication Data

Brown, Marc Tolon.   Finger rhymes.
(A Unicorn book)

Summary: Presents 14 rhymes with instructions
for accompanying finger plays.
1. Finger play—Juvenile literature.
2. Nursery rhymes—Juvenile literature.
[1. Finger play]   I. Title
GV1218.F5B76   793.4   80-11492   ISBN: 0-525-29732-4

Published in the United States by E. P. Dutton, a Division
of Elsevier-Dutton Publishing Company, Inc., New York

Published simultaneously in Canada by Clarke,
Irwin & Company Limited, Toronto and Vancouver

Editor: Emilie McLeod   Designer: Riki Levinson

Printed in the U.S.A.   First Edition
10 9 8 7 6 5 4 3 2 1

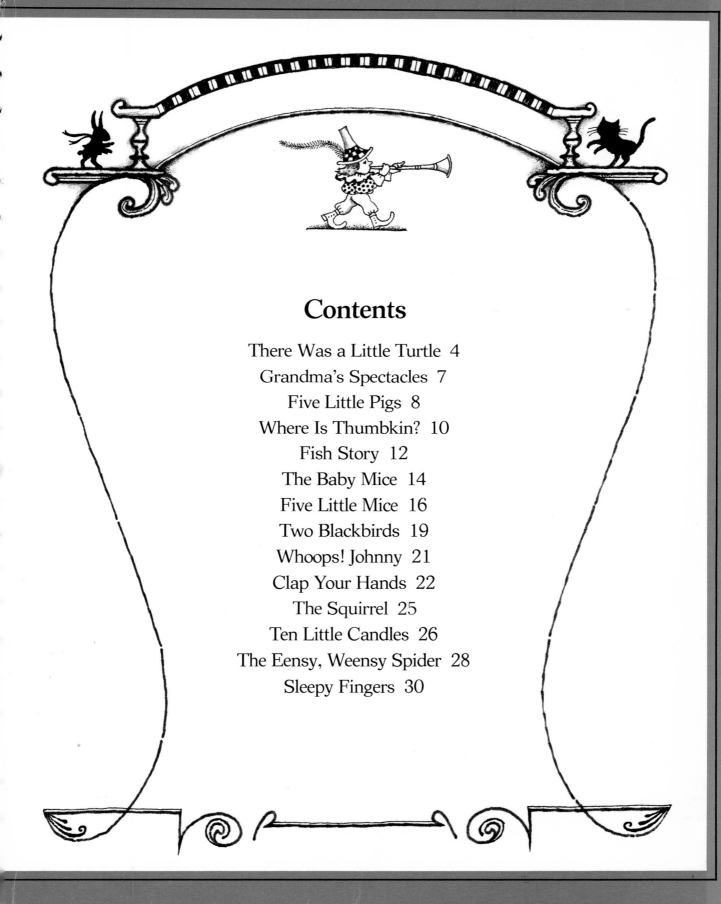

Contents

There Was a Little Turtle

There was a little turtle

 Who lived in a box.

He swam in the puddles

And climbed on the rocks.

He snapped at the mosquito,

He snapped at the flea.

He snapped at the minnow,

And he snapped at me.

He caught the mosquito,

He caught the flea.

He caught the minnow,

But he didn't catch me!

5

Grandma's Spectacles

 These are Grandma's spectacles,

 This is Grandma's hat.

 This is the way she folds her hands

 And lays them in her lap.

Five Little Pigs

 This little pig went to market.

This little pig stayed home.

This little pig had roast beef.

This little pig had none.

This little pig cried "Wee, wee, wee!"

All the way home.

Where Is Thumbkin?

Where is Thumbkin?

Where is Thumbkin?

Here I am, here I am.

How are you today?

Very well, thank you.

Go away, go away.

Where is Pointer?

Where is Pointer?

Here I am, here I am.

How are you today?

Very well, thank you.

Go away, go away.

Where is Tall Man?

Where is Tall Man?

Here I am, here I am.

How are you today?

Very well, thank you.

Go away, go away.

Where is Ring Man?

Where is Ring Man?

Here I am, here I am.

How are you today?

Very well, thank you.

Go away, go away.

Where is Small Man?

Where is Small Man?

Here I am, here I am.

How are you today?

Very well, thank you.

Go away, go away.

Fish Story

One, two, three, four, five—

Once I caught a fish alive.

Six, seven, eight, nine, ten—

Then I let it go again.

Why did I let it go?

Because it bit my finger so.

Which finger did it bite?

The little finger on the right.

The Baby Mice

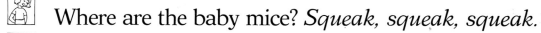 Where are the baby mice? *Squeak, squeak, squeak.*

I cannot see them. Peek, peek, peek.

Here they come from the hole in the wall,

One, two, three, four, five—that's all!

Five Little Mice

Five little mice on the pantry floor—

This little mouse peeked behind the door.

This little mouse nibbled at the cake.

This little mouse not a sound did make.

This little mouse took a bite of cheese.

This little mouse heard the kitten sneeze.

"Ah-choo!" sneezed the kitten,

And "Squeak!" they cried

As they found a hole and ran inside.

18

Two Blackbirds

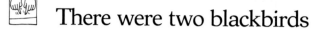 There were two blackbirds

Sitting on a hill—

The one named Jack,

The other named Jill.

Fly away, Jack!

Fly away, Jill!

Come again, Jack!

Come again, Jill!

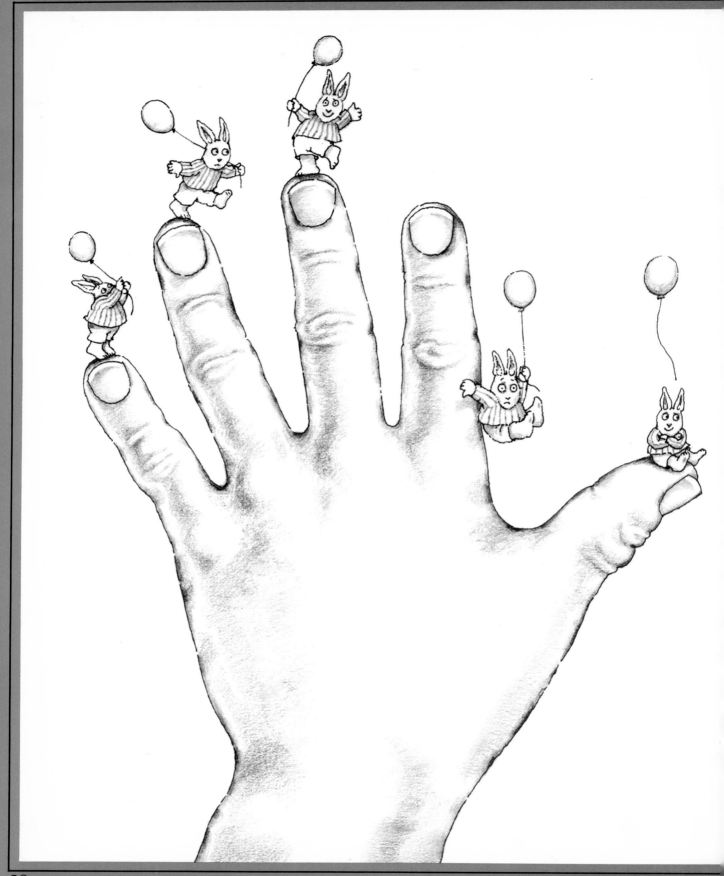

Whoops! Johnny

 Johnny,

 Johnny,

 Johnny,

 Johnny,

 Whoops!

 Johnny.

 Whoops!

 Johnny,

 Johnny,

 Johnny,

 Johnny.

Then cross arms.
(Ask your friend to do it.)

 Now you do it.

(The trick is that most people forget
to cross their arms when they finish.)

Clap Your Hands

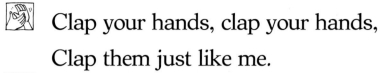 Clap your hands, clap your hands,

Clap them just like me.

Touch your shoulders, touch your shoulders,

Touch them just like me.

Tap your knees, tap your knees,

Tap them just like me.

Shake your head, shake your head,

Shake it just like me.

Clap your hands, clap your hands.

Now let them quiet be.

23

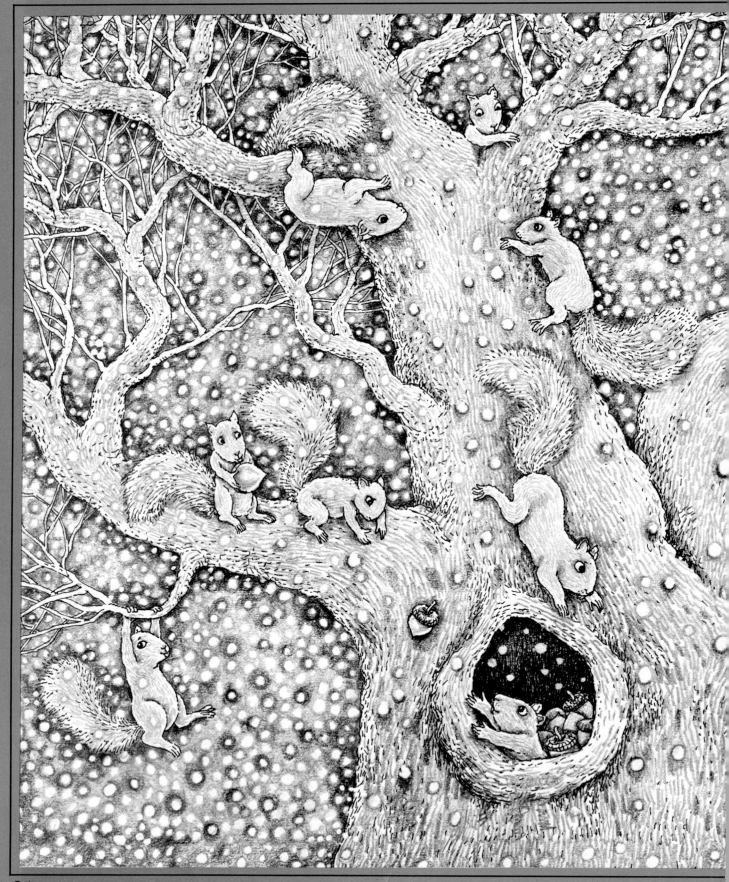

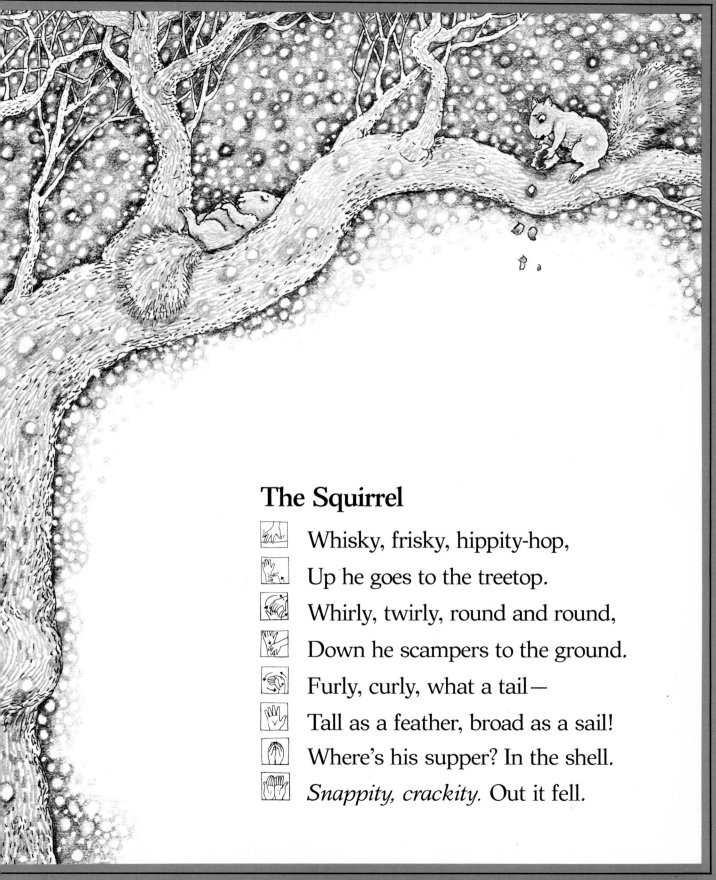

The Squirrel

Whisky, frisky, hippity-hop,

Up he goes to the treetop.

Whirly, twirly, round and round,

Down he scampers to the ground.

Furly, curly, what a tail—

Tall as a feather, broad as a sail!

Where's his supper? In the shell.

Snappity, crackity. Out it fell.

Ten Little Candles

Ten little candles on a chocolate cake.

Wh! Wh! Now there are eight.

Eight little candles on candlesticks.

Wh! Wh! Now there are six.

Six little candles and not one more.

Wh! Wh! Now there are four.

Four little candles—red, white and blue.

Wh! Wh! Now there are two.

Two little candles standing in the sun.

Wh! Wh!

Now there are none!

The Eensy, Weensy Spider

The eensy, weensy spider

Climbed up the waterspout.

Down came the rain

And washed the spider out.

Out came the sun

And dried up all the rain.

So the eensy, weensy spider

Climbed up the spout again.

Sleepy Fingers

My fingers are so sleepy,

It's time they went to bed.

First you, Baby Finger,

Tuck in your little head.

Ring Man, now it's your turn.

Then comes Tall Man great.

Pointer Finger, hurry, because it's getting late!

Let's see if they're all nestled.

No, there's one to come.

Move over, little Pointer,

Make room for Master Thumb!

ACKNOWLEDGMENTS

I am indebted to the Flint Public Library, in Flint, Michigan, for sharing its extensive collection of finger rhymes, from which my son Tucker and I selected our favorites.